W9-AGP-194

# Mystery at Meadowbrook

New edition! Revised and abridged

By Laura Lee Hope

Illustrations by Pepe Gonzalez

Publishers · GROSSET & DUNLAP · New York

Revised and abridged by Nancy S. Axelrad.

Copyright © 1990 by Simon & Schuster, Inc. All rights reserved. Published by Grosset & Dunlap, Inc., a member of The Putnam and Grosset Book Group, New York. Published simultaneously in Canada. Printed in the U.S.A. THE BOBBSEY TWINS is a registered trademark of Simon & Schuster, Inc. Library of Congress Catalog Card Number: 88–82985
ISBN 0–448–09100–3

ABCDEFGHIJ

# Contents

# Contents

*Look for these new*
*BOBBSEY TWINS® reissues:*

# ■ 1 ■
# Bear on the Loose

"I predict you will solve a very, very puzzling mystery at Meadowbrook!" Dinah Johnson said as she and the four Bobbsey children entered the baggage area at Wellstown Airport.

"We will?" Freddie Bobbsey asked. He was six years old with curly blond hair, like his twin sister, Flossie. Turning eagerly toward the older set of Bobbsey twins, he said, "Did you hear that?"

"Dinah's teasing you," Nan replied. She and her brother Bert were twelve and had dark hair.

"No, she's not," Flossie said. "Look!"

She pointed to a wooden crate that stood behind the baggage carousel.

"There's something alive in there!" Freddie cried. "Let's go see what it is!"

"Don't get too close," warned Dinah, who was the Bobbseys' housekeeper. The younger children stood on tiptoe and peeked between the slats of the crate.

1

"It's a baby bear!" Freddie exclaimed.

"Step away now," Dinah ordered, drawing him back. "I promised your mother and father I would look after you on this trip. So think of me as the boss."

"But it's only a baby," he insisted.

"Baby or not, it's still a bear!" Dinah exclaimed, her sable eyes watching the ball of fur inside the crate.

Nan and Bert examined the shipping label. "It's addressed to Mr. T. E. Holden," Bert said. "He owns one of the farms next to Uncle Daniel and Aunt Sarah's farm."

"I wonder why he's getting a bear cub," Nan said.

"And I wonder where your uncle is," Dinah added, putting down her suitcase. "Maybe you ought to call the farm."

Nan ran to a row of telephones near the exit and returned a few minutes later. "Aunt Sarah says Uncle Daniel and Hal left an hour ago. They should've been here by now."

"Here they come!" Freddie shouted as the farm pickup truck pulled to the curb. A blond athletic-looking boy the same age as Bert jumped out. He was the twins' cousin Harry Bobbsey, whose nickname was Hal. He was followed by his tall, rugged father.

"Hey, everybody!" Harry said.

"Hey, Hal!" Bert chuckled, slapping Harry's palm good-naturedly.

"Sorry we're late," Uncle Daniel said as the children greeted each other. "I had to make a stop at the Holdens' farm." He glanced toward the crate. "That's probably what Mr. Holden asked me to pick up, Harry. Help me carry it to the truck."

"We know what's inside!" Flossie shouted. "A baby bear!"

"Why is Mr. Holden getting a bear?" Freddie asked.

"He runs an animal hotel on his farm," Harry explained. He tagged after his father, who signed a receipt for the shipment.

"An animal hotel? Maybe we should send Snap and Snoop there for a vacation," Dinah said, laughing. Snap was the Bobbseys' shaggy white dog, and Snoop was their black cat.

"They would probably have a good time there," said Harry. "People who go on trips and don't have anyone to care for their pets while they're away drop them off at the Holdens'. It's so much better than most kennels. There's plenty of space and lots of fresh air. Mr. Holden says it's like a health resort for animals."

"A health resort for animals!" Dinah repeated. "Now I've heard everything. But what is a bear going to do there?"

3

"The same as the other animals. His owner performed with him in the circus. But she's been sick and has to spend some time getting better before she can travel again."

"All right, big question," Uncle Daniel said. "Who wants to help put Arthur in the truck?"

"Arthur?" Flossie asked.

"That's the bear's name," her uncle said.

"That's a funny name for a bear," Flossie said.

"Maybe they should have called it Freddie," Uncle Daniel replied, the corners of his eyes crinkling. "Now, where are my volunteers?"

"Here!" Freddie shouted, jumping up and down.

"Thanks, Freddie. I think he's a little heavy for you alone. I'll have Harry and Bert help you."

The boys staggered under the weight, but finally managed to lift the crate onto the truck. They put it at the back, next to the luggage, which was lined up along one side.

"May Freddie and I ride in the back with Arthur?" Flossie asked.

"We all will," Bert said.

"Just make sure you don't disturb that bear," Dinah said, getting into the front seat.

"They'll be all right," Uncle Daniel assured her.

"I certainly hope so," said Dinah. "I just know how those children collect trouble."

4

Meanwhile, Flossie, who was fidgety, left the place where she was sitting and crawled beside the crate.

"Hello, Arthur," she said. "You're going to a hotel. What do you think of that?"

Arthur grunted.

"Be careful, Flossie," Harry cautioned. "Some of those slats are loose. He might be able to get his paw out and scratch you. Bears can't pull in their claws the way cats do."

Just then, Arthur grunted loudly.

"Oh!" Flossie gasped and crawled next to Bert.

"Tell us more about bears," Freddie said.

"Well, they have five toes on all four feet," Harry replied. "Cats and dogs have only four toes on their back feet. Bears like to climb trees, and Mr. Holden says most bears can swim too!"

"Can they dive?" Flossie asked. She noticed a look of alarm on Harry's face. "What's wrong?"

"Your pocketbook!" Harry exclaimed.

"Uh-oh," Freddie said.

The little girl glanced at the floor where she had laid her bag. To her surprise, its handle was hooked around Arthur's claws.

"Give that back to me, you bad bear!" Flossie demanded, but the cub paid no attention and dragged the purse closer.

"I'll get it for you, Flossie," Bert said, climbing behind her.

5

At the same moment, the truck hit an enormous hole in the road. Bert skidded into the crate, and the tailgate on the truck sprang open.

"Yikes!" Bert cried as the crate slid off the truck and crashed against the pavement.

"Arthur!" Flossie screamed.

The slats on one side of the crate splintered apart, and the small, furry creature rolled out. He rose on his stubby legs, ran to the other side of the road, and sank clumsily into a ditch.

Hearing the commotion, Uncle Daniel stopped the truck. "What happened?" he yelled. The children leapt to the ground and started after the bear.

"Arthur's loose!" Nan shouted.

By this time the cub had crossed the ditch to a field and discovered a clump of blueberries, which he began to eat.

"Don't go any closer! I may have to lasso him!" Uncle Daniel said, removing a coil of rope from the back of the truck.

Flossie took her sister's hand and watched intently as her uncle approached the bear. When he saw how tame Arthur was, he quickened his steps.

"Okay, fella," Uncle Daniel said, looping the rope under his collar. "Snacktime's over."

"He's really a pussycat, isn't he?" Bert said as he and Harry went to help.

Arthur did not want to leave his meal of berries and planted his four feet firmly on the ground.

"Didn't you hear Uncle Daniel?" Bert said. "You have to go back on the truck." The boys grabbed the rope from Uncle Daniel and pulled the reluctant animal away from the bushes.

At last Arthur gave in and ambled back to the truck, where he was put inside and tied up.

"If I had brought honey along," Dinah said to Uncle Daniel, "we'd have caught him real fast."

"You're right. Too bad I didn't think of that before I left." The farmer chuckled as the truck rumbled forward.

Flossie, who was sitting as far away from the bear as she could, clutched her pocketbook. "He might want to take it again!" she said.

No longer interested in the bag, Arthur laid his head on his paws.

"Something always happens when we come to Meadowbrook," Nan remarked, smiling at the sleepy bear.

"Which reminds me," Harry said. "I forgot to tell you about our mystery!"

"What mystery?" the twins asked excitedly.

8

# ■ 2 ■
# Animal Hotel

"Wow!" Freddie said, his eyes growing wide. "Dinah really did know there'd be a mystery."

All the children held their breath until Harry continued.

"There have been a series of bank robberies in this area," he said. "No one has a clue about who the robbers are."

"I hope they don't come here!" Flossie exclaimed.

"Don't worry. I'll protect you!" Freddie boasted.

Everyone waited for Harry to continue. But he didn't say anything more.

"Is that it?" asked Bert. "I thought you said there was a mystery."

"There *is*," Harry said defensively. "The mystery is that the bank robbers disguise themselves differently each time. No one has a description of what they really look like. And no one has even seen how they get away."

9

"Wellll," said Bert, pretending to be deep in thought, "I guess that *could* count as a mystery. I'll have to wait and see."

"You might get a good chance to see, too," said Harry. "You know, Dad's on the board of directors of the Meadowbrook Bank. They're afraid it's going to be robbed, too."

The truck turned onto a country lane that led past acres of rich farmland.

"Almost home," Uncle Daniel said to Dinah. "Too bad Sam couldn't come along with you. But being the foreman at my brother's lumberyard must keep your husband quite busy."

"It sure does. But we're going to take a vacation at the end of the summer—without a certain four young detectives!"

Uncle Daniel laughed. "How will they manage without you?"

"Poorly," said Dinah. "That's just the way I want it, though. It means I'll always have a job to come back to."

Uncle Daniel laughed again. Then he brought the truck to a gradual stop beside a large white clapboard house. A plump, friendly-looking woman hurried down the porch steps.

"Hi, Aunt Sarah!" Nan called.

"Hello, everyone," her aunt replied, giving each of the twins a hug while Uncle Daniel lowered Dinah's suitcase off the truck. "My goodness. What's that?" Aunt Sarah gasped, noticing the small bear.

"That's Arthur," Harry explained. "We have to take him to Mr. Holden."

"I'm glad to hear it," his mother said. "I doubt Rocket would like having a bear for a playmate."

"Speaking of Rocket, how *is* he?" Bert asked.

"Oh, he's fine. Do you want to see him?" Harry asked. "He's in the barn."

Rocket was the palomino pony the twins' mother had bought for them the last time they visited Meadowbrook. Since they didn't have the space to keep a pony at home, they boarded him at their cousin's.

"Take your suitcases into the house first," Aunt Sarah said.

"Oh, I'll do it, Sarah," said Uncle Daniel. "Let the twins see their pony."

"There's Rocket!" Nan cried, dashing to the first stall.

"Did you miss us, boy?" Bert asked, stroking the pony gently.

"We missed you," Flossie said.

Rocket whinnied.

"Is anyone going to Mr. Holden's besides me?" Uncle Daniel hollered across the yard a little later.

"We are!" the twins shouted.

Arthur sat on his haunches and peered at

11

them sleepily as the children climbed into the truck.

"Arthur looks like he needs a vacation," Bert said.

It was a short ride to the Holden farm, and Harry pointed out the animal hotel as they came to a stop.

"See that kennel with the fence around it?" he said. "That's part of the hotel."

At one end was a big red maple tree, and under it, reclining on a cushion of grass, was a regal-looking dog with long, silky hair.

"Where's the rest of the hotel?" Bert asked.

"On the other side of the driveway," Harry said, waving to a dark-haired boy who had just emerged from the kennel. Harry introduced Mr. Holden's son, Tom, who was a few months younger than he.

"Thanks for bringing the bear cub," Tom said as the cousins carried Arthur off the truck.

"Where is Arthur's room?" Flossie asked.

"Behind the kennel. He'll be staying in our deluxe suite, complete with his very own tree for climbing, and plenty of honey!" Tom grinned and led the visitors to an enclosure surrounded by raspberry bushes.

"Arthur loves berries!" Freddie exclaimed.

The little bear yawned and bobbed his head up and down as if to say yes, then plopped down lazily in the shade.

As he did, music drifted out from behind the trees and Arthur rose on his hind legs and began moving in a circle.

"He's dancing!" Flossie said as a tall, ruddy-faced man emerged with a small tape recorder. It was Mr. Holden.

"His owner taught him to do that," Mr. Holden said. Tom introduced his father. "Welcome to our animal hotel! Why don't we go see the rest of it?"

As he switched off the tape recorder, the children followed him across the driveway.

"This is where we keep the cats," Mr. Holden said. He opened the gate and strode to a gray-blue building with freshly painted white shutters and window boxes filled with pink geraniums. "You won't find a better place for pets to stay," the farmer went on, "unless it's home, of course."

Stepping inside, the twins were amazed to find each cat inside a large cage that looked more like a miniature room. Each cage had a fluffy bed with lots of toys and plenty of space for the animal to stretch and walk.

"Snoop would like this," Flossie said, eyeing a white angora cat. "How do you do?" she asked.

"Her name is Sugar," Tom said.

Sugar meowed.

On the opposite side was an animal with brownish fur. It had a tail with black rings around it and a black stripe across its face that looked like a mask.

"That's a raccoon!" Freddie said. "I saw one when Bert and I went camping!"

"He's the second oddball here, along with Arthur," Tom replied. "His footprints look just like a human's because he walks on the flat part of his feet, not on his toes like other animals."

"He's cute," Flossie said. "Is he somebody's pet?"

"Uh-huh. Do you want to see my homing pigeons?"

"Sure," Bert said. Tom, Harry, and the twins left Mr. Holden and Uncle Daniel.

"See you back at the truck," Harry's father replied.

Tom, Harry, Nan, and Bert went on ahead. Freddie and Flossie heard footsteps behind them and turned to see a tall boy with a scowl on his face stroll into view.

"That's Mark Teron!" Freddie whispered to his twin. "We met him at Meadowbrook the last time we were here."

"He likes to tease us," Flossie said, watching him saunter toward the cat building.

"Where are you going?" Freddie shouted.

Hearing the sound of Freddie's voice, Mark jumped. "So, it's you again! I heard you were coming to visit Hal."

14

"You didn't answer my question," Freddie said, running toward him.

"I want to see the kitty-cats. Any law against that?"

"Why?" Freddie asked.

"Oh, get lost!" Mark said, giving Freddie a shove that sent him staggering into the wire fence.

"Stop it!" Flossie screamed. "Freddie didn't do anything to you!"

Bert, who had heard the ruckus, turned on his heels and raced down the driveway. "Leave my brother alone!" he shouted.

Fists raised, Mark charged forward. "Make me!" he snarled. Bert caught his arm and hurled him to the ground.

Mark tried to get to his feet but stumbled and fell. "Get away from me!" he cried, scrambling to avoid another attack.

"Not until you promise to stop bullying little kids like my brother," Bert said.

Mr. Holden and Uncle Daniel saw the fight and stormed over to where the children were. "Stop this at once!" Mr. Holden ordered.

"Mark pushed Freddie," Flossie said as Mark got to his feet.

"I've already told you once, Mark," Mr. Holden said. "I want you to stay away from these animals. If you can't, don't come here at all!"

"It wasn't my fault," Mark grumbled as the men stalked off to the west field.

Bert watched Mark make a face and kick some dirt off his shoes. "What a creep," Bert said to himself. Then to Mark he said, "You'd better leave before Mr. Holden and my uncle come back."

"I'm going," Mark said with a sneer. "Don't rush me."

As he vanished down the driveway, Bert patted Freddie's shoulder. "Let's go see the pigeons," Bert said to his younger brother and sister.

As the children entered the barnyard, their eyes were drawn to the long flat roof of the barn. On top of the roof was a large wooden box with a wire cage next to it.

"What's that?" Flossie asked.

"That's the pigeon loft. Tom says the birds stay in the wire cage during the day to get sunlight," Bert explained. "But at night they go into their wooden house and sit on perches. Come on. I'll show you."

The children hurried through the barn and up a stairway to the second level. Tom was showing Nan and Harry the bands he had put on the legs of his pigeons.

"These go on when the bird is a week old," Tom said. "It's still possible to slide the ring over the claw when the pigeons are that age."

"What are those markings on the bands?" Nan asked.

"Registration numbers," Harry said. "I've got pigeons also. Both his birds and mine are registered with the Meadowbrook Pigeon Club."

Just then, Bert, Freddie, and Flossie joined the others. They told about what had happened with Mark Teron.

"That's just like him," said Tom. "I wish he'd stay away from here."

"Come closer and see the birds," Nan said to Freddie.

"Do your pigeons ever fly home with messages?" Freddie asked Tom.

"Sometimes."

"What makes them come back?"

"They want to be with their mates and get food and water. Only one of a pair is entered in a race. See this trapdoor?" Tom continued, pointing to a small opening in the side of the loft. "It's set up so the bird can get into the loft but not out of it. He lands on that little board out there and then pushes the trapdoor with his beak."

As he scooped a handful of seed into his palm, a pigeon flew to the boy's shoulder and began pecking at it.

"We never feed the birds until just before the

17

racing pigeons are due back, because we want them to hear the others feeding. That makes them want to get into the loft fast."

"Meadowbrook Pigeon Club is having a race soon," Harry put in. "Tom and I will need somebody to stay by the loft while we take the birds out. Do you want to help us?"

"I do," Bert said.

"So do I," Nan added.

"Great," Tom said, unaware that Flossie had wandered out onto the roof. She circled the wire enclosure to watch the pigeons strutting on the floor.

Suddenly one of them landed on a strip of wire in front of her and she stepped back, startled.

"Help!" Flossie shrieked.

Her small, chubby fingers grabbed at the metal gutter that ran along the roof as her feet slid off the edge of the roof.

# ▪ 3 ▪
# The Chase

When they heard Flossie's cry, Bert and Nan dashed out of the pigeon loft with Tom and the other children. Tom ran downstairs to the barn while the older twins flattened themselves on the roof and grabbed Flossie's wrists.

"Hold on, Flossie!" Nan cried, trying to pull her up.

"Freddie, go get Uncle Daniel!" Bert said.

But as the boy started off, a ladder settled against the edge of the roof and Tom's head rose into view. He grasped Flossie firmly and set her feet on the rungs of the ladder.

"You're okay now," he told her.

She felt suddenly weak but held the sides of the ladder tightly. Nan reached forward to help and saw the stream of tears rolling down Flossie's face.

"You're safe now," Nan said.

"I was scared," Flossie murmured, stepping

onto the roof. "Thank you for saving me, Tom."

"Yes, thank you," Nan echoed as her sister wiped her eyes. "I don't know how much longer Bert and I could've held on."

"I'll bet you could catch the bank robbers, Tom," Harry said as they went downstairs.

"Me?" Tom smiled. He was flattered by his friend's remark. "Not me. I don't know what I'd do if I even saw them."

"I know what I'd do," Freddie said. "I'd sneak up and grab them and yell *'Help!'*"

"And I would help you!" Flossie promised.

"You could run for the police officer," Freddie replied.

"What would you do if you met the robbers?" Tom asked Nan.

She pondered a moment. "I'd make believe I didn't see them. Then I'd run and call the police to come right away!"

"Hal and I wouldn't wait for anyone. We'd take them straight to jail!" Bert said with confidence.

Harry raised his eyebrows. "I like Nan's idea better."

As the children ran from the barnyard, they saw Uncle Daniel seated behind the wheel of the farm truck. "What took you so long?" he called. "We don't want to be late for supper."

After telling about Flossie's near accident, the

twins and Harry said good-bye to Tom and his father and hurried into the truck for the ride back.

"See you later," Tom said, waving to the children as Uncle Daniel tapped his horn.

When they reached Meadowbrook Farm, Aunt Sarah was talking on the telephone. Upon seeing her husband, she handed him the receiver.

"Bad news," she said.

"What happened, Aunt Sarah?" Nan asked.

"The Meadowbrook Bank has been robbed." Aunt Sarah shook her head grimly as the phone conversation ended and Uncle Daniel signaled for silence. He explained that the guard had come upon two men just as they were leaving the bank with several sacks of money.

"Then he knows what they look like!" Harry exclaimed excitedly.

"I'm sorry to say he doesn't," his father said. "Both men had masks on. But he chased them and saw them get into an old green car that was parked next to the bank. It's the first real clue we have."

"Did he see which way they went?" Bert asked.

"No, but the town police did, thank goodness. They were coming to answer the alarm call, when they saw the car headed in this direction."

"Come on!" Freddie said, going to the front door. "Let's set up a roadblock!"

"Freddie, don't!" Aunt Sarah said, too late. All the children had hurried out of the house and down the lane.

"There they go!" Harry cried as an old-model green car sped by with two men in the front seat. "Too bad I couldn't see their faces."

"We've got to follow them!" Freddie said. He ran back to the farmhouse, where Uncle Daniel had been watching from the doorway.

"We saw the robbers, Dad!" Harry said. "They were in a green car!"

"And it looked old!" Bert exclaimed. "Please, can't we go after them?"

"This is a matter for the police," Uncle Daniel said.

"We just want to see where the robbers are going!" Bert pleaded.

Despite the light drizzle that had begun falling and Uncle Daniel's initial reluctance, he and the children piled into the family van and drove down the road.

"There it is!" Bert cried. He pointed to a green speck in the distance.

"Hurry, Dad!" Harry urged.

Daniel Bobbsey pressed his foot on the accelerator, jolting the vehicle forward in a burst of speed. There was no other traffic on the road, which made it easier to keep the robbers in sight. But the drizzle had thickened into heavy rain, and the green car vanished.

"I'll radio the police on the CB," said Harry.

"We'd better go back. The road's getting slick," Uncle Daniel said, slowing the van a bit.

"Don't give up!" Bert said. "We can still catch them!"

"You don't have to call the police, Hal," Nan said. "I see a patrol car coming up behind us. I hope we don't get a speeding ticket."

The police car signaled for Uncle Daniel to pull over to the side of the road. It came to a halt, and a husky dark-haired man in uniform got out.

"Lieutenant Kent!" Uncle Daniel called, rolling down his window.

"Mr. Bobbsey! Where are you tearing along to on this wet road? And"—he peered in the window—"with a van full of kids!"

"The children saw an old green car with two men drive by our farm," Uncle Daniel said. "They thought it might be the bank robbers. I was following it. I realized I was going too fast for this weather, and I was slowing down."

"I was just about to radio you," said Harry.

By this time another state policeman named Bennett had joined Lieutenant Kent. When Bennett heard the story, he relayed the information to headquarters.

"They'll put an alarm out all over the state for

that car," Lieutenant Kent said to Uncle Daniel. "We're fairly sure the men you saw are the same ones who broke into the Meadowbrook Bank and the others."

"Sorry we couldn't catch them," Uncle Daniel said.

"Don't worry. We'll find them," the lieutenant replied.

"*We'll* keep looking, too!" Freddie said, waving to the officers as they drove past the Bobbseys. Then Uncle Daniel drove back home.

"We sure had an exciting day in Meadowbrook!" Flossie commented that night when she and Nan were getting ready for bed.

"We sure did! A bear and pigeons and bank robbers!" Nan said.

"I almost flew away, too." Flossie giggled.

"Well, I'm glad you didn't," Nan said, turning out the lamp. "You could've been really hurt. Good night."

"'Night," said Flossie, the cotton blanket tucked warmly around her chin.

The next morning, right after breakfast, Harry phoned state police headquarters to speak to Lieutenant Kent.

"We didn't find the green car," the officer said, "and we still don't know who the bank robbers are."

As Harry was reporting this to the others, the phone rang. Aunt Sarah answered it and spent a few minutes mostly listening. When she rejoined the children, she had a serious look on her face.

"That was Mr. Holden. His father, who moved to California several years ago, was taken to the hospital during the night. He's doing poorly, and Mr. and Mrs. Holden are flying out as soon as they can."

"Is Tom going, too?" Nan asked.

"They would take him, but they don't know how long they'll be gone. Mr. Holden asked a friend to help Tom look after the animals. But the friend can't come for a few days."

"Can't Tom stay here?" said Harry.

"I already mentioned that to Mrs. Holden," said Aunt Sarah. "But that still leaves the problem of taking care of the animals. I told Mrs. Holden we could drive Tom back and forth, but it's a lot of work for just one boy. Besides, she'd feel better if an adult could supervise him. Your father and I just don't have that kind of time to spare."

Dinah had overheard the news. "Mrs. Bobbsey," she said, "why don't you let me go over there and help Tom take care of the animals? I can look after Tom, too. I'd be happy to."

"That's very generous of you, Dinah. I'll call Mrs. Holden back at once," Aunt Sarah replied.

"I'm sure she'll be delighted with the idea."

The offer was quickly accepted. Dinah went upstairs to pack her bag while Aunt Sarah and the children hurried into the van.

When the Bobbseys reached the Holden farm, Mr. and Mrs. Holden had already left, and Tom was feeding the animals. Aunt Sarah and Dinah went into the house while the cousins accompanied Tom to the cage where Arthur the bear cub was kept.

"Arthur's gone!" Tom said, aghast.

"That's awful!" Nan exclaimed.

"It's worse than awful. Just wait till my dad finds out. He'll be furious."

Flossie slipped her hand into Tom's. "We'll find Arthur for you," she said.

The group scattered and began their anxious search. Nan and Flossie walked up to the orchard while Harry and Bert went to the field behind the barn, and Tom examined the cage for clues.

"Now what would a real detective do?" Freddie asked himself. "He'd look for tracks!"

The little boy wandered slowly up the lane and peered at the ground. Behind the house was a dirt path, soft and muddy because of the previous night's rain.

"Prints!" he exclaimed, bending down to trace the small indentations with his finger. "There are five toe marks and five claw marks. They must be Arthur's!"

Freddie looked around. The other children had vanished. "I'll just have to find Arthur without them!" he said to himself.

He followed the path into the woods until wet leaves covered the telltale trail. All around him were dark towering trees and a maze of fallen limbs.

"I don't think Arthur came this way," said Freddie. He doubled back and looked for the trail. But he couldn't find it. He had no clue which way he should go.

Freddie felt a sinking feeling come over him. "I'm lost!" he said aloud, shuddering.

# 4

# On the Trail

When Freddie realized he was lost, he sat down on a log to think.

"The path just disappeared," he thought anxiously, getting up and pushing back through the bushes. "No, it didn't! There it is!"

Having turned around several times, though, he wasn't sure which way he had come. He noticed his footprints leading off to the right.

"If I don't find Arthur, I guess I'll have to go back," he concluded, trudging on until he saw a small animal sitting in the middle of the trail. It was black with a broad white stripe running down its back and a long bushy tail.

"Hi!" Freddie said, deciding to make friends. A rustling sound came from the bushes and Nan and Flossie appeared.

"Don't touch that skunk!" Nan warned. "It'll squirt on you!"

Freddie turned around. "I thought his tracks

were Arthur's," he said as the skunk scooted down the path. "I guess I was wrong."

Nan observed the paw prints. "They look like a bear's," she admitted, "but these are much smaller."

"Anyway, *we* found Arthur!" Flossie announced. "He was sitting in a tree in the orchard!"

"How did you find *me*?" Freddie asked. "I thought I was lost in the forest."

"You were lost until we found you, silly." Flossie smiled as Nan told Freddie that they had searched everywhere for him.

"We were walking at the edge of the woods when we spotted your red T-shirt," Nan said.

"See? You weren't as far away as you thought," Flossie added. She returned to the Holden house with Freddie and Nan.

Later, back at Meadowbrook Farm, Bert asked Uncle Daniel if he had heard any news of the robbers.

"Not yet, I'm afraid," Mr. Bobbsey said.

"Why don't we take Rocket out for a ride and scout around?" Bert proposed to the other children. "Maybe we'll find some clues."

The group ran to the barn, where Rocket was feeding on a small bale of hay. He tossed his head and neighed as Harry lifted the harness from the wall.

"I hope you finished your lunch," Harry said,

hitching the pony to the cart as Bert took the reins.

"We'd better go on the back roads," Harry suggested when everyone was seated. "Rocket doesn't like traffic."

Crossing the highway to the next dirt road, the horse and cart clattered past rows of vine-covered fences. The children started singing.

Then suddenly Bert shouted "Whoa!" and brought Rocket to a halt. "Hey, everybody, look up there!"

About fifty yards away, parked between the road and the fence, was an old, battered green car!

"Maybe it belongs to the bank robbers!" Freddie exclaimed.

"Let's see. Pull up a little farther, Bert," Harry said.

The boy guided Rocket off the road and the children got down. Cautiously they gathered around the vehicle and peered through the dust-covered windows.

"Money bags!" Nan whispered, pointing to several brown cloth bags on the backseat.

She was about to open the door, when her brother said, "Don't touch anything. We could spoil the robbers' fingerprints!"

Hastily Nan drew back her hand. "You're right," she agreed, looking around. "I wonder where they went."

"I see two men!" Flossie said, gasping. She pointed across the field.

"They must be burying the treasure!" Freddie said, his blue eyes round with excitement. "Let's capture them!"

"Wait a minute!" Bert said. "That's too dangerous. Let's split up and spy on them. We'll keep out of sight, so they won't attack us or run away.

"Freddie and Flossie, you come with me," Bert instructed, tying Rocket's reins around a fence post. "We'll stake out that fence to the right."

"Harry and I will cover the one on the left," Nan said.

After giving the V-for-victory sign, the older girl and her cousin climbed over the fence and walked along the left side. They hid in the shadow of the bushes that divided the fields while Bert and the younger twins hurried in the opposite direction.

"Come on!" Bert whispered to Freddie and Flossie as he cleared the adjoining fence.

Flossie followed quickly, but when Freddie tried to climb over the fence, a jagged section caught in the pocket of his jeans and he hung there, helpless.

"I'm stuck!" Freddie whispered loudly, crying to his sister to come back. She climbed to the top of the fence and released Freddie's pocket.

"Hurry!" Flossie said, running ahead of him.

The trio approached stealthily and saw the two figures move toward a clump of bushes at the edge of the field. They also saw Nan and Harry.

"Uh-oh," said Bert. "I hope the thieves don't see them."

Just then, the shorter of the two figures wheeled about and faced Bert.

"Bud Stout!" Bert exclaimed as the second figure looked up. "And Ken, your brother!"

"Who'd you think it was?" Bud Stout asked. Bud was a schoolmate of Harry's, whom Bert knew from other visits to Meadowbrook.

"We thought you were the bank robbers!" Bert replied sheepishly. "Sorry we scared you."

"Bank robbers! Do we look like bank robbers?" Ken inquired. He was in his late teens.

At that moment Nan and Harry walked out from their cover.

"You, too?" said Bud to Harry. "You also thought we were robbers?"

Harry looked embarrassed, but then Bert reminded Bud and Ken that the Meadowbrook Bank robbers had escaped in a green car.

"Well, this isn't it," Ken said. "I bought mine with the money I earned helping my father."

"Do you mind telling us when you bought it?" Nan asked.

"Last week, so it can't be the one those guys were using. I just hope the police don't make the same mistake you did and try to arrest me."

"When we saw the sacks on the backseat, we thought they were full of stolen money," Bert remarked.

"They're full of blueberries. We picked them for Mom," Bud said.

They picked up their buckets and walked toward the road with the Bobbseys. Upon reaching his car, Ken scooped handfuls of berries into an empty grocery bag and gave it to Bert.

"With our compliments," Ken said, licking his fingers.

"Just imagine if this was the missing loot!" Bud said.

"I like blueberries better," Freddie declared, "'cause we can eat them!"

The Stout brothers got into the car and drove away. Bert untied Rocket. "We might as well go home," he said.

When the pony realized he was headed for Meadowbrook Farm, he trotted faster.

"This is lots of fun!" Flossie said. Her yellow curls blew in the breeze as Rocket trotted briskly up the lane to the farm and came to a stop at the barn door.

"Thank you, Rocket," Nan said, petting the animal as Harry unhitched the cart.

The other children hurried into the house to tell Aunt Sarah about their meeting with the Stout brothers.

"Ken gave us these blueberries," Bert said, plunking the bag on the kitchen counter.

"Tom Holden phoned," Aunt Sarah said. "His father's friend, Amos Berg, arrived earlier than expected. That means Dinah can come back now."

"Hooray!" shouted Freddie and Flossie.

"I'm going to call Tom," said Harry.

When he called, Tom told Harry, "I don't need to stay home all the time and take care of the animals anymore. So how about a practice race tomorrow between my pigeons and yours?"

"Yeah, terrific!" Harry exclaimed. "Nan and Flossie will come over first thing in the morning."

Excited at the prospect, the children planned to meet as early as possible. When Nan and Flossie arrived at the Holden farm, Tom was waiting for them with a pigeon in his wicker basket.

"I don't understand something. How will you know which bird won the race?" Nan asked. "Your pigeon and Harry's don't come back to the same loft."

Tom explained that the birds were released together. As soon as each bird entered its own loft, someone wrote down the exact time. Then the distance of the pigeon's flight was divided by the time it had taken for the bird to fly home. "That's why I need you girls to help me," Tom said.

Tom showed Nan and Flossie where his pigeon would come in.

"You have to wait for the bird to go inside the loft before you write down the time," he said, pointing to a large wall clock. "Harry and I are going to a field halfway between his farm and mine, and we'll start the race from there. Then we'll go back to Meadowbrook. Call us there and let us know how long the bird took."

Nan and Flossie stationed themselves on the flat roof of the barn by the loft. After they had waited nearly twenty minutes, a gray bird settled on the landing platform in front of the trapdoor.

"It's twenty minutes after ten," Flossie said, looking at the clock. "Quick, Nan! Write it down!"

"We have to wait for the pigeon to come inside," her sister protested. She coaxed the bird, but without success.

"Come here, birdy," Flossie pleaded.

Finally the pigeon nudged the trapdoor open and hopped into the loft. Nan and Flossie dashed to the house, and Nan telephoned Meadowbrook Farm to tell Tom what time his pigeon had returned.

"Harry won that race," Tom said, disappointed. "Bert logged the pigeon in at eighteen minutes. We're just on our way over to see you, so wait for us."

As the girls stepped outside, they saw a pigeon fly out of the woods.

"I wonder where that one came from," Flossie said. "Do you think it belongs to Tom?"

After following the mysterious bird a short distance, the girls dashed toward the road and noticed a green car parked at the edge of the woods.

"There's Ken Stout's car," Flossie said. "He and Bud must be picking berries again."

Nan glanced at her wristwatch. "The boys will be here any minute. We'd better go back to the house."

As she had predicted, the boys arrived shortly. Tom introduced them to Amos Berg, a friendly, dark-haired man with slate-blue eyes.

"Hey, here comes Bud," Harry said as the stocky boy walked across the farmyard.

"Hi, Bud!" Nan called. "We just saw your car on the back road."

Bud grinned. "You didn't see our car. It broke down right after we left you yesterday. It's in town being fixed."

Nan looked startled. "Then that must have been the bank robbers' car!" she cried.

# ■ 5 ■
# Bert's Discovery

"The bank robbers!" Freddie exclaimed. "Where are they? Let's get them!"

With the other Bobbseys at his heels, the boy ran to the end of the lane. "Which way?" he asked Flossie.

"Over there on that little road by the woods," she said.

The children darted ahead but stopped as Nan paused to look around. "I'm sure the car was parked here," she said. "But it's gone!"

"Let's look for clues," Bert said.

Inching along, he and the others studied the ground carefully. Freddie got down on his hands and knees to examine the dirt for tire marks, but the ground was completely dry. It showed no evidence that a car had been there.

"I don't see anything," Freddie said.

"Neither do I," Bert added, discouraged. "We'd better go back to the farm."

They reached the house just in time to hear the start of a local newscast on the kitchen radio. "The Meadowbrook Bank, which was robbed two days ago," the announcer said, "is offering a reward to anyone providing information leading to the arrest of the robbers."

"This is exciting!" Flossie said.

As further details were given, the telephone rang and Harry leapt to answer it.

"We sure would!" he exclaimed, clanging the receiver down a few seconds later. "That was Bud Stout! His dad wants us to go camping with them."

"Yippee! I love to sleep outdoors!" Freddie shouted. "When are we going?"

"Tomorrow!"

Aunt Sarah, who had overheard the announcement, smiled. "That's very nice of Mr. Stout."

"He said he'll pick us up at nine o'clock," Harry said. "Tom Holden's going too, and Bud asked Patty Manners and Kim Harold so Nan and Flossie won't be the only girls."

That evening the children went to bed early. Freddie dreamed that a big black bear was nuzzling him in his sleeping bag. He tried pushing the animal away, but it was no use.

"Wake up, Freddie!" Bert said, shaking his

brother. "Everybody else is downstairs waiting!"

Like a flash Freddie was out of bed and tearing across the room, first to his closet and then to a drawer filled with underwear and socks. When Mr. Stout pulled up in his farm truck, even Freddie was set to leave.

"Hi!" called a freckle-faced girl with dark curly hair. It was Patty.

"Isn't this going to be fun?" said Kim, her blond companion. Then she noticed Freddie's feet. He was wearing one red sock and one green one.

"Freddie looks like a Christmas tree," Flossie said, giggling.

"I do not!" he said, his face growing as red as his sock.

After all the children had been introduced, Nan climbed next to Kim and Flossie in the front seat. The rest of the children settled contentedly in the back on two long benches.

"All set?" Uncle Daniel asked, coming out to talk to Mr. Stout. The men's conversation quickly turned to the bank robbers. "Despite the children's clue about the green car they saw, the police haven't been able to locate it," Uncle Daniel said.

"We'd better keep our eyes peeled," Bert said.

Harry gave a mock salute. "Yes, sir!" he replied, chuckling.

"Where are you headed?" Uncle Daniel asked Mr. Stout.

"Oh, I figure Boulder Lake might be interesting. It's a long hike in from the road, but the kids won't mind walking. It isn't far from here as the crow flies, but by truck it'll probably take us most of the day."

"Does the pigeon fly the same way?" Flossie asked.

"I guess a pigeon would take the shortest way, too!" Mr. Stout laughed. "That's what we mean when we say 'as the crow flies,'" he replied, starting the engine.

Waving good-bye to Uncle Daniel, Aunt Sarah, and Dinah—who was now back at Meadowbrook Farm—Bert reminded his companions to start watching for the bank robbers. "If you see anything that looks the least bit suspicious, shout," he said.

All morning and afternoon, the Bobbseys kept a sharp lookout for the green car and the two bank robbers, but they didn't see them.

At about three o'clock the farm truck started up a steep, rocky incline and pulled under a tree.

"This is it. Everybody out!" Mr. Stout called.

"Where's the lake?" Flossie asked, surveying the stony landscape.

"The road doesn't go any farther," Bud told her. "We have to walk the rest of the way."

Each of the campers took a load from the truck and the hike began. Climbing over the rocky ground, they quickly came to dense woods.

"Boulder Lake is on the other side of these trees," Bud said.

"I see it!" Freddie shouted, running ahead of the others.

The lake was surrounded by tall, stately pine trees and boulders that lay randomly on its shore.

"I've never seen so many rocks! Look at all of them!" Nan exclaimed.

"The lake is bee-yoo-ti-ful!" Flossie cried.

"We're pretty close to the top of the mountain," Mr. Stout said. "Meadowbrook Farm is down behind the woods." He pointed to one end of the lake.

It wasn't long before the campers had staked their tents and fixed a tasty meal of grilled hamburgers and hot dogs.

"I'm really glad we came here," Harry remarked, squirting extra mustard on his hot dog.

"So am I," Nan said. "This burger is yummy."

By the time the children had swallowed their last mouthfuls, darkness began creeping over the campsite, and Mr. Stout built a roaring fire.

"I'm going down to the lake," Bert announced. Harry offered to join him.

From where the boys stood on the shoreline, Meadowbrook Farm seemed far away.

"Hey, what's that?" Bert asked, squinting at a fiery glow in the distance.

"Looks like a campfire," Harry said.

"Why would anyone want to camp down there? It's full of rocks."

"Those lights are farther away than you realize. They're much closer to Meadowbrook than we are," Harry replied.

A few seconds later he and Bert heard the others start singing around the campfire.

"It's cold out here. Let's go back," Harry said.

"In a minute." Bert lingered to watch as the light grew brighter. "They must have added wood to the fire," Bert said. Then he and Harry returned to their companions.

Later, as the singing continued, Nan glanced at Flossie. She was fast asleep. When the singing stopped, Flossie got up drowsily and went to her tent.

"'Night." Flossie yawned.

"I suggest the rest of us should do the same," Mr. Stout said.

Except for the crickets chirping in the dark forest, all was soon quiet.

Flossie had fallen into a deep sleep almost immediately, but she awakened when something brushed against her.

44

"Nan!" she whispered. Her sister did not stir. "Nan, wake up!"

"What is it?" the other girl murmured sleepily.

"There's something by my pillow. I'm afraid to move!"

Nan reached for her flashlight and turned it on, directing the light toward Flossie. Cowering next to the girl was a fat little furry animal.

"It's an opossum!" Nan exclaimed as it scurried out of the tent.

"I wish he had stayed!" Flossie said sorrowfully. "I could have played with him!"

"Go back to sleep," Nan said. "It's late."

The next thing they heard was the sound of the boys cooking breakfast.

"We're having fried-egg sandwiches," Bud called. "They're a Stout specialty!"

He tore holes in several slices of bread and put them on a hot griddle. Then he cracked an egg into each hole. When each egg was fully cooked, he flipped the bread over and fried the other side.

"We call these bull's-eyes," Bud said.

"Mine's delicious," Patty Manners said.

The others agreed. For a few minutes the only sounds were those of eating.

Then Bert said to Harry, "Remember those lights we saw last night?"

"What lights?" Nan interrupted.

Her brother explained about the mysterious glow he had discovered on the other side of the mountain.

"We'll be driving back that way," Mr. Stout said.

"Would you mind stopping?" Bert asked. "It occurred to me those lights could have belonged to the bank robbers. I'd like to investigate."

"Bud told me you're quite a detective," Mr. Stout said.

"We like to solve mysteries," Nan said as the camping gear was divided among the children.

Halfway down the mountain road, Mr. Stout told Bert, "Just tell me where you want me to stop."

"Right here is fine."

The truck screeched to a halt.

Within seconds everyone was tramping across the rocky terrain into the woods.

"I see deer tracks," Tom said shortly.

"They look like flower petals to me," Flossie remarked.

"Deer walk on their toenails, like all hoofed animals. That's why the tracks look like that."

"I've found something even more interesting," Bert said excitedly. "Human footprints!"

# ■ 6 ■
# New Suspicions

"Let's follow them!" Nan exclaimed.

There were two sets of prints, one narrower than the other. They led through a small grassy clearing, then back into the woods, where portions of the ground were covered by stone.

"This is where they end. Footprints won't show up on rock," Bud said, observing a large triangle-shaped boulder a few feet away.

"If I could climb to the top, I bet I'd have a good view of the valley," Bert suggested. "Maybe I could see who was here before us."

With Harry's help, Bert found several footholds and pulled himself slowly to the top.

"See anyone?" Nan asked as her brother gazed over the countryside.

"No one." He sighed with disappointment.

"You might as well come down, Bert," Mr. Stout said.

"Yes, sir."

47

Despite the failure of their search, the children were eager to get back to Meadowbrook Farm. Bert and Freddie were seated next to Bud's father, when they saw a patrol car parked sideways across the road.

"A roadblock!" Mr. Stout said.

"Maybe it's for the bank robbers," Freddie remarked.

As the truck approached, they noticed two more patrol cars. One of them was at the far end of the road, while the other stood next to a cornfield. Lieutenant Kent was holding a bullhorn to his lips.

"We know you're in that field! Come out immediately!" the officer roared.

The truck came to a halt and the children hopped out.

"What's going on?" Harry asked, running forward with Bert.

"A man up the road claims he saw two men run into this cornfield," the officer said. "They could be the bank robbers."

Why would they hide in a cornfield? Bert wondered. It's not much of a place to hide. Sooner or later they would have to come out.

Still, the cornstalks were high and leafy, and any number of men could have hidden among them without being detected.

Lieutenant Kent lifted the bullhorn again.

"Just walk out quietly, and no one will get hurt!" he promised, but there was no response.

"Maybe they ran across the field and escaped out the other side," Nan suggested.

"I doubt it," the patrolman said. "We've got the whole field surrounded."

"Hal and I will go in and find the men for you," Bert offered.

"Hey, what about Tom and me?" Bud spoke up.

The officer smiled. "Thanks, boys, but I can't let you do it. It's much too dangerous. The robbers may be armed."

"Can you force them to come out?" Nan asked.

Lieutenant Kent explained that when a certain signal was given, an army of policemen would move into the field from all sides.

As he spoke, three shrill whistles sounded. "That's it," he said, motioning to the other officers to follow him.

"This is scary, isn't it?" said Flossie.

Suddenly the cornstalks began waving back and forth.

"Here comes someone!" Freddie gulped. "Maybe it's a robber!"

While he spoke, five patrolmen stepped into view.

"Didn't you find anyone?" Bert asked, addressing Officer Bennett, who was in the lead.

"No one. We combed that field from every direction," the officer said as Lieutenant Kent came up behind him.

"Either they left before we got there, or they're hiding *under* that field," said the lieutenant. "We might as well lift the roadblock."

Mr. Stout dropped Tom off at the dirt road that led to his farm. Then he drove Harry and his cousins to Meadowbrook Farm.

Harry and the twins had a great deal to tell Uncle Daniel and Aunt Sarah. They had barely finished when they were interrupted by a call from Tom Holden.

"Something terrible has happened!" he told Nan. "All the dogs are gone!"

"Oh, no! How?" she asked as the other children gathered around. "Where was Amos?"

Bert took the receiver. After listening to Tom's story he said, "Who do you think did it?"

Tom explained that Amos had driven to town in the morning to buy more food for the animals. When he returned, he found the kennel door open and the dogs missing.

"I'll bet Mark Teron did it!" Tom concluded. "He's probably angry because we told him to stay away from the animals."

"You really shouldn't accuse Mark unless you have proof," Bert said.

"I'm not going to wait for proof," Tom said defiantly. "I'm going to call him and ask him about it right now!"

When he called back a few minutes later, however, he had changed his tone. "I guess I was wrong. Mark's mother said he left early yesterday morning to visit his grandmother for a few days."

"So Mark couldn't be responsible. Did you notify the police?" Harry asked.

"Amos called headquarters a little while ago."

"Tell Tom we'll be over tomorrow," Bert put in.

When the phone conversation ended, the children discussed the puzzling turn of events. Had the dogs been stolen or let loose? Why hadn't the other animals also been taken? Now there were new unanswered questions.

Next morning the Bobbseys quickly helped Harry with his chores and then headed to the Holden farm. When they arrived, Tom was leaning wearily on the mailbox at the end of the lane.

"The police came last night, and they stopped by again just now," he announced.

"What do they think happened?" Bert inquired.

"They're not sure. They say either somebody opened the kennel and let the dogs go loose, or else they were stolen."

"Wouldn't the animals have come back on their own if they could have?" Nan asked. "This is where they get fed."

"Good point," Tom said, "assuming they weren't left too far from here."

"Let's see what *we* can find," said Nan.

The ground beyond the kennel gate was so badly trampled it was impossible to distinguish prints of any sort.

"If the dognapper ran into the woods, we ought to look there too," Harry remarked.

In spite of a thorough search, the young detectives found no clues in the woods.

"Any more ideas?" Tom asked dolefully.

"We haven't been inside the kennel," Freddie said.

He went to the entrance and examined the long line of empty cages. At least they were intact.

"We might as well give up," Tom said.

"We can't!" said Bert. "Not yet." The others agreed.

The children started down the road toward the next farm and saw the mail carrier putting letters in a mailbox.

"Hello," he said pleasantly as Tom approached.

Tom explained about the missing animals. "I was wondering if you saw any of them when you were out yesterday," he said.

"No, but I did see an old beat-up truck going lickety-split down the road. I waved to the driver to slow down. He nearly ran me over."

"Do you remember the license plate number?" Nan inquired.

"Sorry. I didn't even get a look at it."

Tom seemed more miserable than ever as the children went back to the Holden farm. "Just because you've solved other mysteries, it doesn't mean you can solve this one," he said to the twins. "Maybe I'd do better if I tried to find my dogs myself!"

# ▪ 7 ▪
# Barge Mishap

Shocked by Tom's sudden outburst, Nan said, "We were only trying to help. Maybe you're right, Tom. Maybe *you* can solve the mystery by yourself."

Tom's eyes welled with tears as he broke away from the group and ran down the road.

"Tom!" Harry called.

"Let him go," Bert said. "He's just upset, but he'll get over it."

The children went back to Meadowbrook Farm. When he noticed how quiet they were, Uncle Daniel led them into the living room to talk. "You all look so unhappy," he said. "Do you want to tell me what happened?"

"Tom wants to solve the mystery all by himself!" Flossie said sulkily.

"He doesn't want us to help him!" Freddie blurted out as the older twins told how the dogs had vanished from the animal hotel.

"Tom will probably be sorry about the way he acted," Uncle Daniel said. "I've got an idea, Harry. You know my friend Bill Taylor? He's the one who gives barge rides on the old canal for tourists. Why don't you get a group of your friends together and take the trip tomorrow? If everyone helps extra hard around here, your mother and I can go too."

"That sounds wonderful!" Nan said.

"What's a barge?" Flossie asked.

"Barges are flat-bottomed boats," her uncle explained. "In the old days they used to carry freight and passengers up and down the canals."

"I read about one in a book. Barges don't have engines," Bert added. "They're pulled by mules that walk along the canal bank."

"Call some of your friends, Hal," his father suggested. "I'm sure Tom would like to go."

"You really think so?" Harry asked, unconvinced.

"I do."

To the boy's surprise, Mr. Bobbsey was right. Tom apologized for his outburst and happily accepted the invitation along with Patty, Kim, and Bud.

"They'll meet us at the dock," Harry said. "Bud's brother is going to drive them."

"I don't know whether I can go with you guys," Freddie spoke up. "I really want to find the robbers."

"We'll have a chance to look for them while we're on the barge," Bert assured him. "A good detective looks for clues wherever he goes. Uncle Daniel says the canal runs through some back country, and the robbers could very well be hiding there."

The next morning Freddie was the first to climb into the van.

"Aren't you coming, Dinah?" he shouted.

"No," said Dinah. "I've had my fill of boat rides for a while." Earlier that summer, she had joined the twins and their parents on a house-boat trip.

"Who wants to skin the mules?" Uncle Daniel asked as Aunt Sarah got in after the other children.

"Skin them? That's mean!" Flossie said with a frown.

"Oh, it's not as bad as it sounds," her uncle answered. "A mule skinner is the person who drives or rides the mule."

"That's different!" said Flossie, greatly relieved.

When they reached the canal dock, they found the others waiting for them. Tom shifted awkwardly.

"Hi, Tom!" Bert called cheerfully as Tom stuck his hands in his pockets.

On a grassy bank behind him two mules

grazed peacefully. The barge, low and rectangular with a striped canopy spread over the top, was tied to a nearby post.

"Who wants to ride the mules first?" Aunt Sarah asked.

"I do!" Bert cried.

"So do I!" said Nan.

"Okay, you two," Uncle Daniel said, "your mules are named Peanuts and Popcorn. The lead mule is Peanuts."

The animals were hitched together, one behind the other, with a rope that was fastened to the barge.

"You take Peanuts, Bert. I like Popcorn," Nan said, mounting her mule as the other children settled on benches along the sides of the barge.

At once the barge edged out into the canal with a loud groan. Shaded by trees that grew over the embankments, the water was a dark, inky blue.

Uncle Daniel sat in the rear, his hand on the large iron handle of the boat's rudder.

"It's so quiet," Kim said as they glided along.

Listening to the rhythmic *clop-clop* of the mules' hooves, Harry said, "Speed it up, Peanuts and Popcorn!"

"What's your hurry?" Bert asked as he and Nan dug their heels into the animals' flanks.

"No rush!" said Harry.

"Good, 'cause these mules aren't in a hurry either!" Nan said.

The animals plodded along the worn path, stopping from time to time to nibble leaves on bushes, and the rope grew slack.

"Come on, Peanuts!" Bert urged.

With a quiet snort, the mule stepped ahead. But the rope caught on a piece of iron pipe sticking out from the bank. It looped around tightly, forcing the animals to back up.

"I'll loosen the rope," Nan said, leaning down. Popcorn twisted around to see what was happening. Nan lost her balance and fell off Popcorn's back. She tumbled into the canal right in front of the barge.

"Nan!" Aunt Sarah screamed.

Uncle Daniel pulled the rudder hard, trying to swing the boat away. "Move!" he shouted to Nan, but it was no use. Nan was much too stunned. The barge was heading straight for her!

"I'll get her!" Harry cried, jumping into the shallow water and seizing her by the arm.

"Oh, Hal!" she said, stumbling up the embankment. "I was so scared. I just froze."

"Are you all right?" Aunt Sarah asked as the children climbed aboard.

"I'm fine, thanks to Hal," Nan said. She sat on

the bow, out from under the canopy, and let the sunshine dry her hair and clothes.

"It's time for someone else to skin the mules!" Bert announced as he slid off Peanuts and joined his sister. "That was a close call," he said to Nan, offering her his windbreaker. "Here. Put this on if you start to feel cold."

Tom and Kim were next to ride the mules, and the barge trip continued peacefully.

After a while, another dock came into view. Uncle Daniel instructed Tom and Kim to slow the mules. The barge slowed down too, and Uncle Daniel jumped off. He tied the mules to posts along the dock.

"There's a nice picnic area just on the other side of the dock," said Aunt Sarah.

"How about if we go for a hike first?" said Bert. "I'm not hungry yet."

"A Bobbsey not hungry? I can't believe it," said Uncle Daniel. "But if you want to go for a walk, take fifteen minutes. In the meantime the rest of us will set out lunch. That is, if everybody else isn't going along with Bert."

Bert looked around. Only Bud decided to join him.

The two boys soon disappeared along a trail through the trees.

"Don't get lost," Freddie called to them. "You don't want to miss lunch!"

The boys walked along the cool trail, watching birds fly from tree to tree and listening to the sounds of animals scampering out of their way. Suddenly Bert stopped.

"Listen!" he said. "Footsteps! This way!"

Directly ahead of them was a man, his face hidden in the shadows. He looked back over his shoulder and saw the boys, then began to run. Bert and Bud followed.

Suddenly Bud tripped over a tree root and fell onto the cool ground. "We've lost him!" the boy moaned as Bert hurried to help him up. "And it's all my fault!"

"We couldn't have caught him anyway," his companion replied.

"You know, this area looks familiar," Bud said. "I'm sure I've been in these woods before. We're not very far from the Holden farm, are we?"

"I guess not," Bert said.

"There used to be an old log cabin around here. Maybe that guy we saw is living in it."

"A cabin? Show me."

A doubtful look spread over Bud's face. "I haven't been here in a long while. I don't know if I can."

"Try," Bert said. "It's important."

The young detectives continued through the woods but saw no sign of a log cabin.

"If we don't go back soon, your aunt and uncle will be worried," Bud said.

"I'll explain everything," Bert answered, reluctant to end the search.

He persuaded his friend to go on until they came to a patch of open field. Near the edge was a small rustic cabin. "There it is!" Bert cried. "I knew we'd find it!"

As the boys approached, they could see that the cabin was badly run-down. The door was hanging on one hinge, and glass had been knocked out of the windows.

"No one could be living here now," Bud said. "The place is ready to fall down."

Bert walked to the door and glanced inside. There was no furniture in the room, and the floor was covered with dead leaves and dust. Indeed, it looked as if no one had been inside for a long time.

"I guess there aren't any clues here." Bert sighed and went around to the back of the building. Here the ground was damp, and Bert noticed two sets of footprints. He bent to examine them.

"Bud!" he called. "Look at these prints! They look like the ones we saw on our camping trip. One set is really narrow!"

"The campsite isn't too far from here. The mountain is on the other side of these woods."

"I realize these prints could have been made by any hiker," Bert said. "But why did that guy run when he saw us?"

"Maybe he thought *we* were the bank robbers," Bud joked.

"Or . . . perhaps he's one of them," Bert said. "Maybe the police have a description by now. I'll try to find out."

With Bud in the lead, the boys made their way back. But when they reached the canal, they weren't at the dock.

"We must be farther down the canal than I thought," Bud ventured.

The boys jogged along the towpath until the dock came into view. Beyond it, they could see the picnickers already hard at work polishing off their lunch.

"Hey, save some for us!" Bert called out.

"Where have you been?" Nan inquired, biting into a ham-and-cheese sandwich.

Bert swallowed. "We saw this guy in the woods. When he saw *us*, he started running. We chased him, but he got away. Then we found this abandoned cabin. . . ."

Bert suddenly caught a glimpse of his uncle, who had a sour look on his face. "I'm really sorry we took so long," Bert said.

"Bert, I know how much you want to catch the bank thieves. We all do. But I don't want you taking foolish risks. Besides, you were gone much longer than you said you would be. I expect you to keep your promises."

"Yes, sir."

"Be sure I don't have to talk to you about this again."

Bert went over and sat quietly with the other children. He told Harry and Nan that Bud had recalled once seeing a log cabin in the woods. "We went to find it. I thought maybe it was being used as a hideout, but it couldn't be."

"What makes you so sure?" Tom said.

"It's too run-down," Bud answered. "There isn't a window in the place."

"It's also empty," Bert added.

"Did you find anything else?" Harry asked as his mother opened a picnic basket and handed sandwiches to Bert and Bud.

"Thanks, Aunt Sarah," Bert said, munching hungrily as he described the footprints he had found. "They looked fresh."

"So someone *has* been at the cabin recently," Nan said.

"Very recently," her brother emphasized.

Convinced that the footprints belonged to the robbers, the children talked of nothing else on the homeward journey.

As they were getting off the barge at the end of the ride, Tom came up to the twins. "I'm sorry about yesterday," he said. "You can help me find the dognappers if you want to."

"Oh, we do," Flossie said happily.

"Shake?" Tom extended his hand to Bert.

"Shake," Bert said with a smile.

All the Bobbseys waved good-bye and piled into the van. On the road back to Meadowbrook Farm, a patrol car blinked its high beams at the van. Uncle Daniel saw them in his rearview mirror. He stopped the car and pulled over. The police officer drove up behind him.

"Mr. Bobbsey, the bank in Rosedale has just been robbed!" the policeman said.

# ■ 8 ■
# Capsule Clue

"Another bank robbery! Officer—" Bert said, but the officer walked away before he could say any more.

"What did you want to ask him?" Uncle Daniel inquired.

"If they have a description of the robbers. Also, I wanted to tell him about the footprints Bud and I saw. I'd like to call headquarters when we get back to the farm—if I may."

"Of course you may."

Back at the farmhouse Bert placed his call. Although information was sparse, the police lieutenant told Bert, "One of the men is stocky. The other one is quite thin. They got away in a green car, so we assume they're the same two who robbed the other banks. The footprints you saw near the cabin could belong to the men. Then again, they might not."

When Bert reported this to the other children, they all wanted to start searching for the robbers immediately.

"Let's go over to Tom's house and check on the rest of the animals," Nan suggested. "Maybe on the way we'll see the green car and the two men."

The walk proved uneventful. When the children started up the Holdens' driveway, they saw Tom crossing the yard with the beautiful white angora cat in his arms.

Flossie ran toward him. "I'm glad they didn't take Sugar," the little girl said, petting the animal.

"I'm glad too," Tom said as a frisky, black-haired dog trotted out of the kennel and barked at the cat.

"That dog!" Freddie said. "Was he one of the missing ones?"

Tom nodded. "Amos found him sleeping on the porch this afternoon. His hair was loaded with burrs."

"He must've been in the woods," Nan said. "Have any of the other dogs come back?"

"No, only Licorice."

"Why don't we go down to that back road again?" Bert proposed after Tom had put the cat in her cage. "The thieves may have left behind some evidence."

While Freddie and Flossie stayed with Amos

at Tom's house, the older children hiked across the highway and into a field. At the end of it was a long dirt road.

Bert slowed his pace. The ground was dry, and the small, deep valleys of mud showed no recent tire marks.

"How about taking us to the cabin you found?" Harry asked. "Maybe we could use it to camp out in sometime."

"You wouldn't want to camp in *that* cabin," said Bert. "You could wake up one morning with the roof on your head. Now which way is the canal?"

"To the left."

"Okay, let's go there first." Bert turned and began picking his way through the underbrush until they came to a winding footpath.

"Are you sure we're going in the right direction?" Nan asked as they headed deeper into the forest.

Her brother indicated a little brook gurgling beside the path. "There was a stream near the cabin, so I figure this has to be part of it," he said, following it until it branched off. "Now where do we go?"

"How about right?" Harry suggested. "There aren't so many trees."

A little farther along, Bert paused again. "There's the cabin!" he cried.

Nan and the boys ran forward. "Hey, this is terrific!" Harry said admiringly.

Tom pushed the sagging door and led Bert and Harry into the one-room cabin. While they looked around inside, Nan looked outside.

She saw a flash of metal gleaming in the sunlight and bent down to pick the object up. It was an aluminum capsule about three-quarters of an inch long, fastened to a small clamp.

"Look, I found something!" she said, studying it closely.

The boys stuck their heads out a side window. "What is it?" Bert asked.

"I don't know." Nan displayed the capsule.

"It's a pigeon message capsule," Tom replied.

"What's that?" Nan asked.

Harry said, "When a pigeon carries a message, it's folded up and put into a tiny container like this one."

"Let's see if there's anything inside," Nan said, pulling the capsule apart. "Zero! And I thought I had found a good clue," Nan said.

"Maybe you have!" Bert said. "How did this capsule get here?"

The children looked at each other and shrugged.

Unable to answer his own question, Bert pocketed the capsule. Then he and his three companions started back along the same path toward the Holden farm.

"All we have are tiny bits of a very big puzzle," Nan said. Bert agreed.

Suddenly Tom stopped. "There's something moving in those bushes," he whispered to Bert, who was behind him.

Nan and Harry froze as Tom put a finger to his lips and crept silently forward. The rustling sound grew louder and a snout poked between the leaves.

"Doxie!" Tom exclaimed, pushing the bushes aside to claim a small brown dachshund.

The dog yelped happily and licked Tom's face as he stooped to lift her up.

"I wonder if the other dogs are around here, too," Nan said.

In the distance the children heard noisy barking. Doxie pulled away from Tom and bounded into the woods.

"Wait for me!" Tom cried.

He dashed after the animal until they reached a small ravine and Doxie had to stop. She gazed across the ravine and barked.

"Over there?" Tom panted. This time the dog howled.

Instantly Tom scooped the animal into his arms and began making his way down the ravine until he was on the other side. Nan and the other boys followed.

By now the distant barking had ceased, and Doxie whimpered.

"Show us where they are, Doxie," Nan said.

The dog lowered her head and sniffed the ground, and the search continued.

"We must be a long way from your farm," Bert said to Tom.

"It only seems like a long way," Tom said. Then he paused as Doxie stopped again. With one paw raised, she perked up her ears. "She hears something."

The dachshund cut across a footpath that led to a stand of pine trees. The children could see the highway beyond it.

Then several dogs appeared, and Doxie and Tom raced to join them.

"Let's give them a chance to calm down," Bert advised his sister.

Except for one bruised paw and some matted fur, the animals appeared to be in good condition. They all knew Tom immediately and jumped around him.

"The dogs won't hurt you," he called to the other children, who had kept a cautious distance. "They're happy to see me, that's all."

He petted the dogs until they quieted down, and then led them back to the Holden farm. When he got them back, he realized that a gray poodle, a prize show dog, was missing.

"If the dogs could talk," Nan said, "they could tell us what happened. Maybe they even know where the other dog is!"

"Someone must've let them out on the highway," Tom remarked. "I hope the missing one didn't get hit by a car."

Upon seeing the other children with the dogs safely in tow, Freddie and Flossie hurried outside with Amos.

"Doxie's the real hero," Tom said, telling the story of the animals' rescue.

"I'll give her a nice juicy steak bone right after supper," Amos said.

"All the dogs will probably want double helpings of dinner," Tom replied.

As everyone stood around enjoying the children's success in finding the dogs, Harry suddenly raised his hand to his forehead. "I almost forgot," he said. "Tomorrow's the big pigeon race!"

"That's right," Nan said. "We have work to do."

As previously agreed, Nan would go to the Holden loft to clock in Tom's birds.

"And I'll be waiting at your loft," Bert said to his cousin, "to welcome the winner!"

"I want to see the pigeons start!" Flossie insisted.

"I do, too!" Freddie added.

"Okay. You'll both ride with me to the starting point," Harry said.

"Good!" Flossie said.

The next morning, after Nan had left for the Holden farm, Freddie and Flossie climbed into the van. They sat in the back. Harry got in the front seat with his wicker basket and held it on his lap. His father, who had offered to drive them to town, stuck his head in the open driver's door. He said, "Put the basket on the floor behind you, son."

Harry squeezed the basket between the two front seats. As he did, the latch released, the basket popped open, and the pigeons flew up into the air!

# ■ 9 ■
# Pigeon Warning

"Close the door!" Harry yelled as he grabbed one of the birds that was flapping over his head.

Uncle Daniel slammed the door immediately, while Freddie put his hands around a bird perched on one of the middle seats. "I caught a pigeon!" he cried.

"Whew!" Harry gasped, returning the two birds to their basket. "I hope they didn't hurt their wings," he said anxiously.

"One of them lost a feather," Flossie said, holding up a long white one that had fluttered into her lap. "Can a pigeon fly without it?"

"No problem," Harry said. "Maybe he'll even go faster!"

Uncle Daniel got into the van and started it up. A short time later, they arrived at a small park in the center of town, where a crowd had begun to gather. Besides Harry and Tom, there were four other contestants, all members of the

Meadowbrook Pigeon Club. They held their pigeons in wicker baskets like Harry's and stood near the starting point.

Tom ran to greet Harry and the twins. "You're late!" he said. "I thought maybe you weren't coming!"

"There's still time till the race is supposed to start," said Harry. "We were held up a few minutes when the pigeons got loose in the van."

"Your birds are probably exhausted," Tom said gleefully, "which means mine will beat them"—he snapped his fingers—"like that!"

"They weren't flying around so long," said Harry. He frowned as Mr. Grimes, the starter, called the contestants together and explained the rules.

"How soon will we know who wins?" Flossie asked.

"Come back here at four o'clock, and I'll announce the winner," Mr. Grimes replied.

A moment later he blew a whistle, and the sides of the baskets were opened. Out flew the pigeons.

All the birds rose into the air. Except for one of Harry's pigeons, they all flew rapidly in the direction of their lofts. It alone circled overhead.

"Whistle and clap your hands!" Harry said.

Freddie put two fingers between his teeth and

blew a piercing blast as Flossie clapped her hands. At once the pigeon stopped circling and headed off toward the farm.

In the Holdens' loft, Nan waited for Tom's two pigeons to return. When she saw them flying toward the barn, she glanced at the clock on the wall. The birds had made excellent time.

"Come on, come on!" she called as they finally pushed through the trapdoor.

After jotting the time on a piece of paper and giving them food and water, she rushed back to Meadowbrook Farm to find out the results of her cousin's team.

"Well? How did they do?" she asked Bert.

"One pigeon came in fast," he said. "The other one isn't here yet!"

Nan blinked in astonishment. "What could have happened to it?"

"I don't know. Harry says the birds sometimes are blown off course."

"But there's hardly any wind today," Nan said.

When Harry returned and heard the news, he said gloomily, "I hope nothing has happened to my other pigeon."

After lunch Uncle Daniel offered to take the racing results to the pigeon club headquarters.

"May the best pigeon win!" he said as he drove down the driveway. "Good luck, everybody. See you later."

"I want to start training my young pigeons right away," Harry said. "Come on!"

The children went out to the loft. Like Tom's, it was built on the roof of the barn.

"What are you going to do first?" Nan asked.

Harry pointed to several birds roosting on wooden slats. "Those pigeons are a month old," he said. "Watch."

He shooed them from their perches and waved his arms to keep them flying about the loft. "This strengthens their wings," he said. "Bert, you take a couple of the birds and show them how to come through the trapdoors."

"I'll help you," Nan offered.

The twins set the pigeons on the landing platform, opened the doors, and pushed the birds inside. After repeating this often enough, the pigeons learned to come in by themselves.

"Now let's try a couple of short flights," Harry proposed. "Ready?"

"May Freddie and I do something?" Flossie asked.

Her cousin picked up two birds and handed them to the younger twins. "Here. These pigeons haven't had anything to eat today. Take them over by the house and let them loose. They'll fly to the loft for food. Meanwhile, I'll start feeding the other birds. That ought to bring these babies back *really* fast."

Freddie and Flossie felt important as they

walked toward the farmhouse, cuddling the pigeons firmly in their arms.

Bert and Nan helped fill the feeders, and soon all the birds were eating. Then came a whir of wings. One bird, then another hopped through the trapdoors.

"Flossie and Freddie did a good job," Bert said as another bird arrived.

"They did a great job. I thought they had only two birds when they left," Nan remarked.

"This is my other racing pigeon!" Harry exclaimed.

"Did you put a capsule on his leg?" Bert asked.

"No. I wonder where this capsule came from." His cousin stared in amazement as Freddie and Flossie came back to the loft.

"What's the matter?" Flossie asked. When she heard that the missing pigeon had returned, she too stared at the message capsule. "Open it! Quick!"

Harry carefully removed the small container from the bird's leg and looked inside. There was a tiny piece of paper folded up tightly.

"Let me take it out, please!" Freddie begged.

Harry handed him the capsule. "Don't rip it," he said as the boy pulled out the paper and handed it back.

Harry scanned the short message and read it

aloud: "'Keep your pigeons out of the woods. And stay out yourself! Danger!'"

Saying "danger" made Harry gulp.

"Who put the note in the pigeon's leg?" Flossie asked.

"That's another mystery to solve!" Bert said. "I don't understand how someone could have done this."

"Whoever they are, they want to keep us out of the woods," Nan concluded worriedly. "Do you think the bank robbers wrote this?"

Bert shrugged. "The only thing I am sure of is, it wasn't written by Danny Rugg."

Danny was a classmate of the older twins who tried to make trouble for them whenever he could. But he was, as far as they knew, many miles away, in Lakeport.

"Be serious," Nan said. "Remember that message capsule I found near the cabin?"

"Yes, but no one was there," Bert argued, "and besides, why would Harry's pigeon have landed so far from home?"

"Sometimes a homing pigeon stops at another pigeon loft," Harry said.

"I didn't see any loft at the cabin," Nan said. "But I guess we ought to go back and look again."

"Not me," Flossie said. "I'd be too scared to go into the woods now."

"Chicken," Freddie teased.

"None of us should go there without a policeman," Nan stated. "Uncle Daniel would probably send us home if he found out."

At that moment Aunt Sarah called across the yard. "Don't you want to find out who won the pigeon race?"

"Let's go in the pony cart," Harry said to the other children.

It took only minutes to hitch Rocket to the cart. When the children reached the park, Mr. Grimes was already there along with the other contestants and their friends.

"It gives me great pleasure to announce the winner of the first race of the Meadowbrook Pigeon Club," he said with a happy grin.

"Who is it? Who is it?" Flossie asked excitedly.

"The winner is"—he paused dramatically to look at all the eager contestants—"Harry Bobbsey of Meadowbrook Farm!"

"Hooray! Hal won!" Flossie squealed as her cousin stepped forward to applause.

Beaming with pride at the small gold-colored trophy that was presented to him, he held it high for everyone to see.

"I hope you win next year, Tom," Harry told his friend later.

"Don't they give a prize to the pigeon?" Freddie inquired.

"I'll give him some extra birdseed," his cousin promised. "He deserves it!"

Freddie nodded his approval.

As the Bobbseys climbed into the pony cart once more, Nan suggested taking the back way. "I know it's a little farther, but it's so much prettier."

In the bright afternoon sunshine, Bert directed Rocket down a country road that rolled gently through the emerald-green valley.

"I'm glad your pigeon won the race," Nan told Harry. "I just wish Tom's could've won too."

"Well—" Harry started to answer as Rocket reared up violently.

Biting his lower lip, the boy clung to the side of the cart to keep from falling out. Bert drew the pony to a halt.

"What happened?" Nan asked.

"I saw something shiny in those bushes back there. It must've scared Rocket," her brother explained.

At once Harry jumped out of the cart and hurried up the road to investigate. "Wowee! Wait till you see this!" he shouted excitedly.

# ■ 10 ■
# Pigeon-Loft Detectives

When they heard Harry's call, the twins scrambled out of the pony cart and ran to where he was standing. There, almost entirely hidden by the bushes, was an old green car.

"The bank robbers' car!" Bert exclaimed. "The door handle must have caught the light and frightened Rocket!"

"Do you think the robbers are around here?" Flossie asked, glancing nervously over her shoulder.

"I don't know," Nan said, "but we ought to contact the state police right away! We're not far from the Holden farm. Let's phone from there."

They arrived at the farm and made the call. In a short time Lieutenant Kent and Officer Bennett arrived. The lieutenant said they would follow the pony cart to where the green car was hidden.

Upon reaching it, Lieutenant Kent took a notebook from his pocket. In it was a description of the bank robbers' car. He compared it with the car in the bushes.

"This is it, all right," he said, observing a dent on the rear fender. "Good work, kids!"

"Rocket found the car!" Freddie said as both officers searched for further clues.

"Let's check the trunk," Officer Bennett suggested. The rear compartment was locked, but it did not take the policemen long to pry open the lock.

"Nothing in here," Lieutenant Kent said, peering inside, "except a spare tire and a bag of grain."

"Grain! What kind?" Harry asked. He examined the bag and exclaimed, "This is pigeon feed!"

With a rush of excitement Nan turned to the officers. "We think the bank robbers may have a pigeon loft somewhere in the woods." She told about the warning note on Harry's pigeon.

"Pigeons, eh?" Lieutenant Kent said.

He went to his car radio to report the children's discovery and received another startling announcement.

"Another bank has just been robbed, about fifty miles from here," the lieutenant informed the young detectives.

"Do you know if they were the same robbers?" asked Nan.

"No one is sure," said Lieutenant Kent.

"Maybe they're different guys," said Harry. "After all, how could they rob a bank fifty miles away if their car is right here?"

"Good point," said Bert. "But they could have used a different car."

"This mystery is getting more and more confusing," said Nan. "And to think that when we came to Meadowbrook, we wondered if there was a mystery at all."

"Well, we'll try to get to the bottom of this," said the lieutenant. "Meanwhile, we'll have this green car towed to headquarters as evidence. There's no need for you to wait."

When the children returned to Meadowbrook Farm, they told Aunt Sarah and Uncle Daniel about their latest adventure. The couple listened in astonishment.

After supper Harry confided to Bert, "I'm really worried."

"About what?" Bert asked.

"About my prize pigeon. Maybe the bank robbers have a friend in the woods who keeps pigeons."

"So?"

"'So'! What if he tries to steal mine," Harry said. "Bert, help me guard the pigeon loft. We won't tell anyone except Mom and Dad."

Although Bert couldn't help but think Harry was overreacting, he agreed, and the boys received permission. They decided to go out to the barn after the other children were asleep.

When Freddie heard footsteps going past his door that night, he got up to investigate. Seeing Bert and Harry in their jeans, he asked sleepily, "Where are you going?"

"Go back to bed," Bert said.

"I don't want to," his brother objected.

"Okay, put some clothes over your pajamas. We're going to the barn to guard the pigeons."

When Freddie had dressed, the three boys went quietly downstairs and crept through the kitchen. Harry stopped for a bowl, which he filled with birdseed when they got to the barn.

"We might need it if we have to rescue a pigeon," he said.

"In that case, I'm going to put some in my pocket," said Bert.

As they lay down in the sweet-smelling hay, Freddie said, "I'm not sleepy anymore. Tell me a story, Bert."

"How about a ghost story?" Harry interjected.

Bert told about a haunted house where doors slammed and lights turned on and off mysteriously. He was just coming to the end, when Uncle Daniel's voice rose from the barnyard.

In the same instant Freddie pointed a shaky finger toward the corner of the haymow. Two large eyes were watching them intently!

"Who—who is it?" Freddie quavered.

"I don't know," Bert whispered. He was about to call out when Uncle Daniel spoke again.

"Is Freddie up there?" he asked.

"Yes, Dad, he's here," Harry replied, as a big bird flew past the boys and out the window. "Those eyes we saw belong to that owl!" Bert cried.

"You should have told us you were taking Freddie," said Uncle Daniel. "Harry, your mother and I were really worried when we found him gone. Come back to the house, all of you."

"But we have to guard the pigeons," Harry said.

"I'm sure the birds will be just fine," his father answered.

Sheepishly the three boys descended the ladder.

"We're sorry," Bert said.

"Just get a good night's sleep," his uncle replied. "The pigeons will be fine."

The next morning, as Uncle Daniel had predicted, the pigeons *were* fine. Freddie and Flossie went off to play in the orchard with Snoop while Nan helped Aunt Sarah and Dinah make raspberry jam.

"How about helping me train the pigeons?" Harry asked Bert. "I'd like to take two of the babies on a practice flight."

"I'm ready!" Bert said eagerly.

Carrying the wicker basket to a nearby field, Harry said, "This is the farthest I've taken these birds. Their mates are back in the loft, so they'll want to return there."

He selected an area where the ground rose to a slight peak, and laid the basket down. "We won't be able to time them, but at least I can see if they fly home."

As the boys knelt beside the basket, a strange pigeon suddenly landed on the lid.

"Where did he come from?" Bert asked. "He isn't one of yours."

Harry picked up the bird. "No, he couldn't be mine. He doesn't have a registration band."

"He has a capsule on his leg!" Bert said.

"That's weird. He's a carrier pigeon, but he isn't registered. I wonder why." Harry took a closer look and added, "His wing is injured. I guess he couldn't fly any farther."

"Let's open the capsule and see if there's a message inside," Bert said.

"Okay. Maybe we can deliver it."

Harry detached the tiny cylinder from the bird's leg and Bert opened it. "There *is* a message!" Bert cried, fumbling as he removed a small wad of paper.

"Hurry! Let me see it!" Harry said.

Bert spread the paper on top of the basket. Printed in block letters were the words: *Every*

89

*girl raves about boys.* Below them was a multiplication exercise: *21 × 100.*

"It's a joke," Harry said, clearly disappointed.

"If it is, I don't get it," Bert said, tapping his cheek. "You know, it could be a secret message in code!"

"From whom?"

"The bank robbers!"

"But the police said they left," Harry remarked.

"Maybe they came back. You're the one who said they could have a friend here who keeps pigeons."

"Well, even if the message is from the robbers, what could it possibly mean? It sounds pretty dumb to me."

Bert studied the paper from all angles and held it toward the sun.

"There's nothing unusual about this paper," Bert said. "I'm sure I was right the first time. These words are a code for some other message."

# ■ 11 ■
# Rescue Route

For several minutes the two boys pored over the writing, but they were unable to decipher its meaning. Finally Harry gave up. "You figure it out if you can. I'm going to send my pigeons home."

"Slow down. We were going to look around the cabin again," Bert reminded him. "Let's do it now!"

"Now?" Harry said.

"Why not?" Bert asked Harry. "Is something bothering you?"

The thought of going back to the cabin made Harry extremely nervous, but he didn't want to tell Bert. "Nothing's bothering me," he said. Then Harry had an idea. "I know something we can do. We can put the capsule on one of *my* pigeons and send it home!" He started to open the wicker basket.

"We can also put a note for Nan on your other pigeon, telling her about the message and asking her to try to decipher the code," Bert said. "We'll let her know that we're going to the cabin and that we'll be home as soon as we're done."

"What if she doesn't go to the loft to get the messages?" Harry asked.

"If she doesn't, she doesn't. We'll just have to hope she does," Bert said encouragingly. He took a small notepad and the stub of a pencil from his shirt pocket and wrote the message.

Harry wound the paper around one of the bird's legs and secured it with a rubber band that Bert also produced from his pocket. Then Harry attached the capsule to the leg of the other pigeon and let both birds go.

"What about the injured pigeon?" Bert asked.

"I'll take him with us and fix his wing when we get home," Harry replied, lowering the bird gently into the wicker basket. "Ready?"

"Ready!" his cousin replied.

The boys walked across the field, entered the woods, and made their way through the underbrush until they came to a footpath. They trudged on in silence. After several minutes the path grew narrower.

"I hate to say it, but I think we're lost," Harry said.

Bert would have agreed, except that a few yards farther along, the path joined another one.

"This looks like the same path Bud and I took when we found the cabin," Bert said.

Following his hunch, the hikers took the second path. They came to a clearing at the edge of which was the deserted cabin. They ran to the door and looked in. The floor was still covered with dirt and dead leaves.

"No one has been here," Harry said.

"I guess not," Bert responded. He was disappointed.

Harry set the pigeon basket on the ground. The bird moved about restlessly.

"I'd still like to know where that pigeon came from," Bert said. "Let's scout the woods."

The two boys explored the area in a widening circle until they lost sight of the cabin entirely. Once again they were in the shadow of the forest. The injured pigeon began cooing and flapping its wings.

"There must be other pigeons around here! Listen!" Harry declared as a faint fluttering sound erupted to the left.

"Something's under those branches!" Bert whispered. Leaves crunched underfoot as he stepped forward.

In the next instant he and Harry were seized from behind!

In the meantime, at Meadowbrook Farm, Nan had decided to check on the pigeon loft. She

climbed to the roof and noticed two pigeons outside the wire enclosure. They were pecking at stray bits of seed on the floor. One of them, she observed, had a piece of paper wrapped around its leg.

I wonder where that came from, Nan thought. She removed the rubber band and read Bert's message. "Oh!" she gasped and quickly unfastened the capsule from the second pigeon.

Nan hurried to find Freddie and Flossie. After telling the twins about Bert's note, she took the message out of the capsule and read aloud: "'Every girl raves about boys.'"

"What does 'rave' mean?" Flossie asked.

"Well, it sort of means to be really enthusiastic about something."

"Oh," Flossie said.

"Bert and Harry are teasing you, Nan," Freddie said.

"No, they're not. Bert thinks this is a code written by the robbers. When somebody wants to send a secret message, he might use one word to stand for a different word so no one else can figure it out."

All three studied the paper until Nan finally said, "Maybe 'every' means a five-letter word beginning with $e$."

No matter how hard they tried, though, none

of the children could come up with anything that made sense.

"Lunch is ready," Aunt Sarah interrupted. "Tell Bert and Harry."

Nan reported her brother's sudden decision to go to the cabin.

"Your uncle has a board meeting at the bank and won't be home for a while," Aunt Sarah said, glancing at her watch. "Who knows what happened to those boys. I'd better call the police."

Within minutes of her phone call, Lieutenant Kent and Officer Bennett arrived at the farm. Nan showed them Bert's message.

"Can you take us to the cabin?" the lieutenant asked.

"Yes," Nan said.

"Good. Then let's go."

Having seen the worried look on Aunt Sarah's face, the lieutenant assured her the children would be carefully guarded. "At this point, they're the only ones who can help us find your son and nephew."

"I know," said Aunt Sarah. "It's just that they take wild chances sometimes."

"They won't with us around."

At Nan's direction the patrol car finally pulled to a stop along a country lane where a path jutted into the woods.

"This way," Nan said, taking the hands of the younger children.

Keeping close together, they pushed deep into the forest until Freddie cried out, "I see the cabin!" They ran inside and were surprised to find no one there.

"The boys must be around here somewhere," Nan insisted. "Bert said they were going to the cabin."

Officer Bennett pushed aside bushes and underbrush. Freddie meanwhile had noticed a squirrel nibbling at a small pile of grain.

"That's pigeon feed," the boy observed, announcing his discovery. "Bert put some birdseed in his pocket last night," he told the others. "Maybe he dropped this."

"He left us a trail!" Nan exclaimed. "See, there's some more!"

"If it is a trail, your brother's a clever boy," Officer Bennett said admiringly.

Although the trail of seed disappeared at times, more was eventually found, and the search went on.

Nan, who saw the boys before anyone else, let out a joyful shout. "I see them!"

Bert and Harry were tied back to back against a tree and had rags stuffed in their mouths. The officers removed the ropes and helped pull the rags out of their mouths.

"I guess you found my trail of birdseed," Bert said, rubbing his arms.

"You bet! That was smart thinking," Lieutenant Kent said. "Now tell us what happened."

Bert and Harry explained how they had been captured while looking for pigeons. Two men, one of them rather tall and thin and the other heavy, had tied the boys up and run away.

"Did they say anything?" Nan asked.

"The thin guy said, 'We have to get out of here fast. We'll pick up the loot and meet the boss tonight,'" Bert remembered. "That's it, word for word."

"They've got to be the bank robbers," Officer Bennett said. "I think we finally have a chance of finding them—and the money they stole."

When the children were back at the farm, Bert asked his sister if she had been able to decode the message.

"I wish I could say yes," Nan said. "Let's all try again."

The children took a pad of paper and some pencils and went to the dining room table.

"Maybe the first letter of each word means something," Bert suggested. He jotted them in big letters: EGRAB.

"E grab! I grab!" Flossie chanted.

Bert looked discouraged as he and Nan rearranged the letters.

"Bert!" Nan said excitedly. "That first word

98

you came up with—'egrab'—spell it backward."

"*Barge!*" Bert exclaimed.

"Couldn't that be a clue?"

"Of course, the canal barge!"

"The men are going to meet the boss there!" Harry cried as his father appeared in the doorway.

"But what about the rest of the message, 'Twenty-one times one hundred'?" Nan asked.

"Maybe that's how much money they stole," Freddie offered.

"No, that's only twenty-one hundred dollars. Besides, why would they write it that way?"

"Wait a minute," said Bert. "Today's the twenty-first. And twenty-one hundred could be the time—that's nine P.M. in military time."

"I bet you're right!" shouted Harry. "The robbers want their boss to meet them at the barge at nine o'clock tonight!"

"What's all the excitement about?" Uncle Daniel asked.

Harry recounted the day's events and the mysterious message he and Bert had retrieved from the pigeon.

"I'll call Mr. Taylor, the barge owner," Mr. Bobbsey said, "and he'll know if anyone has been on it."

Bill Taylor reported that the barge had been safely moored to the dock for the night. He had seen no one near it.

"All the same," Uncle Daniel said, "I think I'll call the police."

"And tell them what?" said Mr. Taylor. "That your nephew figured out a coded message?"

"That's exactly right," said Uncle Daniel. "The kids have provided the only clues about the bank robbers, so I don't see why we shouldn't."

Uncle Daniel hung up and then phoned police headquarters.

"Ask the police if we can meet them at the barge," said Bert.

"I'll be going against my better judgment," said Uncle Daniel, "but okay."

He relayed Bert's request and got permission, but only, the police said, "if everyone keeps out of sight."

By the time Uncle Daniel and the children reached the canal road, the sky had darkened. They crossed a recently plowed field.

"It's a shame there isn't an easier way to get to the canal," Uncle Daniel said as they forged over the rough terrain. Through the trees and bushes that grew along the embankment, they could see the dim outline of the boat.

"There are lights on the barge!" Bert exclaimed.

One light glowed steadily on the bow while another swayed back and forth on the dock.

"Someone's there!" Nan said, her pulse racing.

# ■ 12 ■
# Surprising Solution

Seeing the mysterious light, Uncle Daniel said, "Stay behind me."

He moved cautiously and staggered back as a figure loomed in the darkness.

"Halt!" a man's voice commanded.

"Who are you?" Uncle Daniel asked the man, who was about the same height and weight as he was.

"I own this property and that boat," came the gruff reply. "You're trespassing. Get out!"

"We will not!" said Uncle Daniel. "I know the owner of the barge. You're not Mr. Taylor."

"What of it?" said the man. "You still don't belong here, so get lost."

Uncle Daniel was clearly stalling for time. "We *are* lost," he said. "I figured I could find the barge, and then we could get home from there."

Suddenly the children heard footsteps in the brush behind them. Everyone turned around to see two police officers.

"Mr. Bobbsey, who's your friend?" said one.

"He's no friend of mine," Uncle Daniel said. "But I do think he's a friend of the bank robbers."

The man started to reach under his jacket, but the officers stopped him. While one of them slipped handcuffs on the man and read him his rights, the other one whispered something in Uncle Daniel's ear. He nodded his head.

"Listen, kids," he said. "The officer wants me to pretend to be this man they have in custody. They want me to get the robbers to come off the barge—if they're there. The police will have the dock surrounded."

Uncle Daniel slipped on the prisoner's jacket and cap. The children watched as he walked toward the dock.

"Hello, there!" Uncle Daniel boomed in his deepest voice. A flashlight beam caught his face as he turned away.

"We've got the cash," a man shouted from the barge. "Is everything ready?"

"He thinks Dad's their partner!" Harry whispered.

"Yes! Bring what you've got!" Uncle Daniel yelled gruffly.

Two men stepped off the barge onto the dock. One was tall and thin. The other was of medium height and stocky. Each of them carried a heavy sack over his shoulder.

Upon reaching shore they paused. The heavier man adjusted his sack.

"They're the guys who tied us up!" Bert said.

Suddenly the woods were dotted with tiny light beams moving swiftly in the robbers' direction.

Out of the woods came Lieutenant Kent and several other officers. They swooped toward the robbers and handcuffed them on the spot.

"That takes care of them," said Uncle Daniel. "You children sure helped the police solve this case."

"We're taking the prisoners to the Meadowbrook jail, along with the one we got back in the woods," Lieutenant Kent told the children. "I suggest you come in tomorrow to make a formal identification. Thanks again."

He said good-bye and led the two handcuffed men to the waiting patrol cars.

"So that message *was* for their boss, telling him they hid the money on the barge," Nan said.

"Wait a minute," said Bert. "If the third guy is the boss, and *we* got the message, then how did *he* know when to show up?"

"You're right," said Nan. "There must be a *fourth* guy. I'll bet that the guy they got here was the one who was sending the pigeons out with messages."

"I'm going to call police headquarters and tell them what we suspect," Bert said.

"To think the robbers never knew their boss didn't get the message," Harry added with a chuckle. "And that *we* cracked the code!"

"But how did they send the warning on Harry's racing pigeon?" Flossie asked.

"Tomorrow we'll find out exactly what happened," Bert said.

"I can't wait!" Nan said.

Early the next morning Uncle Daniel drove the young detectives to state police headquarters.

"I heard how brave you were last night," the desk sergeant said, greeting them. "The men confessed to all the bank robberies. They operated out of a location in the woods, but when anyone came there, they hid on the barge."

"How did they get around without their car after they ditched it?" Bert asked.

"They traveled on foot at night. They also stole a truck, which they abandoned."

"I'll bet that was the truck the mailman saw," Nan commented.

"How did the pigeons figure in, and where were they kept?" Harry asked.

"The third guy we brought in was in charge of the pigeons," the sergeant said. "He found your stray pigeon and sent you that message in the capsule. Obviously you didn't take his warning."

Just then Lieutenant Kent stepped into the room. "Good morning," he said to the children. Then he continued telling the story. "You will all be interested to know we found the robbers' pigeons. We let them loose one by one and tracked them in a helicopter. They took us right to the head man. Now he's in jail, too."

"What about the dogs that disappeared from the Holden farm? Did the robbers have anything to do with that?" Bert questioned.

"They saw the sign for the animal hotel and figured maybe they could pick themselves up a guard dog," said Lieutenant Kent.

"But why did they take all the dogs?" asked Nan. "That was a mean thing to do, especially abandoning them in the woods. One dog is still missing."

"Exactly," said the lieutenant. "These robbers are mean through and through."

The children and Uncle Daniel followed Lieutenant Kent into another room, where they stood behind a one-way window and identified the two robbers and their pigeon-keeping friend.

"What creeps!" Harry commented as the children returned to the farm. "I'm going to call the other kids and tell them how the mystery was solved."

After lunch Bud and Tom arrived with Kim and Patty. Bert told the story of the capture.

"Oh, you're all so clever," Kim said.

"And very brave," Patty added.

"I didn't tell you," Tom said, frowning, "that there's still one dog missing. My mom and dad are coming home next week, and they're going to be really upset about it. It was a blue-ribbon show dog!"

The children stopped talking as they heard a car engine humming in the driveway.

"Who's that?" Nan asked as a tall gray-haired man stepped onto the porch.

"It's Mr. Crane. He's the president of the Meadowbrook Bank," Harry said as Aunt Sarah and Uncle Daniel let the visitor inside.

"Mr. Crane has something to tell Harry and the twins," Uncle Daniel said.

"Is it a surprise?" Flossie asked.

"Yes, and a happy one too," Mr. Crane replied with a twinkle in his eyes. "Perhaps you know that Meadowbrook Bank has been offering a reward for the capture of the men who robbed it.

"Our board met this morning," the bank president continued, "and decided it should be given to the five Bobbsey children!"

"Oh, that's wonderful!" Nan said. "I know what we should do with some of the money. We should give it to Tom for the owner of the missing dog. It's not the same as having the dog back, but it's the least we can do."

At that moment the phone rang. Aunt Sarah answered it and talked for less than a minute before rejoining her family and guests.

"That was Amos Berg," she said. "And he has good news. That missing dog has returned, and she doesn't seem the worse for wear. Of course, Amos will have her checked out by the vet. But she's awfully lucky, and so is Tom's family. Something like that would be bad for business."

"Now all the mysteries are solved," Flossie said happily.

Bert looked thoughtful. "I don't know," he said, "if I like it better when we've just solved a mystery or when we have a new one to solve."

Bert would soon have a chance to consider that question some more. Before long, he and the other twins would be in the middle of the exciting *Big Adventure at Home*.